AMISH ROMANCE: AMISH BABY SURPRISE

AMISH BABY COLLECTION BOOK 4

SAMANTHA PRICE

D1519421

CHAPTER ONE

Remember ye not the former things,
neither consider the things of old.
Isaiah 43:18

*F*or Abram, there was no greater thrill than hearing the delighted squeals of his sisters when he returned home.

It had been a long buggy ride from the Gingerich farm and he was exhausted, but when he heard the excited cries of Edith and Sara from a distance, a surge of energy raced through his body.

Even Harry, his best friend and companion on the

day-long journey, had perked up. The horses picked up the pace, and a few minutes later, they arrived at their destination. Abram had been on *rumspringa* for just over a year, and then had spent two months with Harry Gingerich's family, before returning home.

When the buggy finally stopped in front of the barn, Abram's brothers, Luke and Matthew, were quick to ditch the last of their chores to tend to Harry's horse. Edith and Sara ran to meet Abram, and their lively giggles turned into a dozen questions about his travels.

Abram's mother, Ruth, leaned out of the doorway and watched for just a moment, before calling out, "You two have fine timing! Dinner's nearly done. Come on in and wash up, both of you."

Dinner was a fine spread; Abram's mother and his sister-in-laws had clearly been hard at work all day. Abram sat with his brothers and Harry on one side, while his sisters-in-law sat with Edith and Sara on the other. His father led the prayer and, after the 'Amen,' the dishes were passed around.

"Hard to believe it's been over a year already,"

Abram's mother said. "We're so glad you came back to the community."

Abram looked up at his mother to see tears well in her bright, blue eyes. "I know, *Mamm*. I know. That's where I belong, back here in the community with my family."

"Glad to hear it," Abram's father said. "Tomorrow, I expect you'll reacquaint yourself with our cows and chickens. If they could be said to miss anyone, it was you."

Edith chimed in, "The big hen took a chunk out of Luke's boot just the other day. I told him and told him..."

"That's quite enough." Luke playfully wagged his fork.

"Anyway," Abram said. "I'm glad to be back home. I'm sure the Gingerichs will be happy to have one less mouth to feed too."

Harry snorted. "It's a wonder you even came to stay, knowing how my mother cooks." Both boys shuddered at the mutual memory. Harry continued, "Mrs. King, if I could stay here and eat your cooking forever, I think I'd be the happiest man in the world."

Ruth laughed brightly. "Well then, maybe I ought to send Edith along with you, hm? She's better at it than I am."

Harry went a bright red and looked away, muttering something under his breath. Abram elbowed him playfully and tucked into another bite of bread. Edith, pretty, young and blond as she was, went red in her cheeks. Abram had to fight the urge to laugh again, the sight was so comical.

Abram's father leaned back a little in his chair, and worked the cloth napkin between his fingers. "Anything memorable happen at Harry's *haus*?"

"Well, their chickens aren't nearly as ill-tempered." Abram gave a sidelong look to Harry, which caused Harry to laugh.

"Our cows aren't half as sweet, either. Fair trade and all," Harry added.

"But, *nee*, nothing really memorable. Lots of work, and not a whole lot of time to go off to get into trouble. Mr. Gingerich's just as much of a taskmaster as you are, *Dat*." Abram glanced at Harry, and Harry admirably fought down a grin that threatened at the corners of his mouth.

Harry added, "Ayuh, sir. Not even enough time to eat while sitting down most days."

"Well, then," Ruth said. "You'll really enjoy having a nice sit down breakfast before you go in the morning, *jah?*"

"*Jah*, ma'am," Harry said.

"How are your *bruders* doing, Harry?" Mr. King asked.

"All three married off now. *Dat's* scarcely got enough land to split between 'em." He shrugged. "But, he's seeing to make a deal with the Connors just up the way. Come next summer, I think we'll have a lot more land, and more pigs."

"Mm." Abram's father hummed. "Summer after next, we'll be doing the same, I'd say. We're cramped enough in here, but when Abram marries the Hershell's girl, that should give us more than enough land to get a proper dairy going."

Abram prodded listlessly at his dinner, quietened by the recollection that they were trying to make him marry the Hershell girl.

Abram's mother leaned in and whispered, "I know you aren't too keen on it, but that's how it is. You've

SAMANTHA PRICE

had your *rumspringa,* now it's time to think about your responsibilities to the family and to *Gott.*"

"I know, I know." Abram shifted uncomfortably in his chair. He didn't dare look up to see whether his father was looking at him. He could almost feel the man's judgment weighing on him. The young man blew out a breath and continued to pick at his dinner, but his appetite had long gone.

"At least they're only a half day away," Abram's brother, Luke, finally said. "You'd be able to visit more, and we could visit too."

Their father sat back and sucked his teeth for a moment. "Maybe that's what we'll do. Send you, Matthew, and Hannah along next year to work there for a while. Make sure the match will be a fine one."

Abram grimaced a little, but nodded all the same. "Sounds good to me."

Harry nudged him hard. "If you don't take to her, then I just might."

Harry's comment sparked a heated debate between the two young men over which of them would be the better match for Flora Hershell. It was between Harry with his dusky skin, brown hair and eyes, or

6

the gray-eyed and blond Abram. In the end, there was no victor. The good-humored Luke announced he would take a second wife, and laughter erupted around the table. The laughter slowed when Abigail, Luke's wife, did not think it so funny. She sat with her back straight, and her mouth set in a straight line in her pale face.

Edith jumped up and announced she made the dessert. She placed a pink berry confection on the center of the table. While everyone tucked into the dessert, everything settled into a comfortable rhythm, and Abram was glad to be home among friends and family.

WITH ANOTHER PAIR of hands around, things were easier at the Kings' farm. The chickens had clearly calmed down, though Abram suspected they weren't any meaner or sweeter than before he'd left. Abram's presence meant that his sisters were free to learn more of sewing, mending, and cooking. It wouldn't be long before Edith was promised off to someone, maybe even his friend Harry. The Gingerichs had always been a fine family after all.

Abram didn't care to think of marriage much. In truth, he did his best to quash what few memories he had of the past year or so. *Rumspringa* had been a time where he didn't have to think twice about the *Ordnung* or his Amish community and the responsibilities of being a member. In the *Englisch* world while on *rumspringa,* he'd had the freedom to do as he wished. He knew why many young people never returned from their *rumspringa* keeping away from the demands of the community. After a year living as an *Englischer,* Abram felt he'd had enough, and couldn't wait to get back to the community and his family.

He'd had a good time at the Gingerich's farm. It was a good time, almost perfect; Harry's father had let them have free run of the farm after chores were done, unlike his own father. They kept their fair share of alcohol at the Gingerich house, and the boys were allowed to imbibe within reason - and sometimes beyond. Usually beyond, if Mr. Gingerich was already well into his supply. Not so at the Kings' household. Alcohol was not looked on so freely, and neither was anything else. Abram had been brought up strictly, without many privileges that other boys in the community enjoyed.

Abram knew it was best to bury the freedom he'd had on *rumspringa,* and the freedom he'd enjoyed at Harry's house, lest he say or do something of which his father didn't approve.

Even though his family was strict, Abram was glad to be back. He was amazed at how much his sisters had grown, and how much older his brothers looked. At some point while he had been gone, his brothers had become proper men, and he wasn't sure what it was that had done it. Maybe, that's what the burden of responsibility would do to a person. Abram wasn't sure if he felt hopeful or was dreading the responsibilities of adulthood.

Or, maybe, it was just taking on the family farm that made him nervous. Luke and Matthew had often spoken of having their own farm and how good it would be. Abram had never fared well under pressure. He didn't mind the hardship of work and chores, but he could see the frown on his father's face when the bills came in, and Abram never wanted to face that kind of responsibility. The heavy farm work did well enough to keep his mind off such thoughts.

After a while, farm work became a comfortable anesthetic for most things; better to focus on milking those cows, collecting the eggs or feeding the pigs. Better to lose himself in the patterns of farm life. There was the harvest to come, and no doubt there would soon be barn raisings. There would be plenty to occupy his hands, and hopefully, at the same time, his mind.

CHAPTER TWO

But the fruit of the Spirit is love, joy, peace, longsuffering,
gentleness, goodness, faith,
Galatians 5:22

*I*t was some months later when another buggy rolled up to the Kings' house. The passenger got out, and the buggy drove off without waiting. Abram was in the middle of hauling a bucket of feed to the chickens when he heard it.

"Abram King! To the house. Now!"

Abram winced at the sound of his father's angry voice. It was a tone rarely heard from the typically soft-spoken man. His father had used the tone once before, when he and his brothers had gotten themselves into some trouble at a neighbor's orchard. They'd nearly gotten themselves killed that night, and then had regretted coming home to face their father. That was the first and last time Abram recalled hearing his father's anger. Abram dumped the chickens' food on the ground, and went to see what he'd done to upset his father. The chickens had no choice but to wait for their feed.

It was just his mother and father in the living room, or so he had thought. When he rounded the corner, he saw another person, a young woman with dark hair and green eyes. Her braids were mostly tucked up under a kerchief that matched her dress, and that dress strained over the swollen curve of her belly. She sat with her head down, and tears streaked down her cheeks. Her hands were laced together in her lap, and she shook under some unknowable burden. Abram's mother sat in one corner, her face buried in her hands, while his father stood somewhere in the middle.

"Do you know this girl?" his father asked.

Abram shook his head mutely, looking from his father to the pretty young brunette, and back again.

"You will answer me, Abram. Do you know this girl?" his father repeated, with grit in his voice.

"*Nee*, I do not." His tongue felt thick and strange in his mouth. "*Nee,* sir, I do not."

"Her name is Ida King, she says." His father glanced at the girl, and she nodded in silent agreement.

"She tells us that she knows you very well."

"Well, I don't..."

His father cut him off. "She says the child is yours."

Abram choked.

"She also says that you two were married while you were in Virginia." His father's tone soured. "Is that true? Is any of that true? You'd do well to tell me."

Abram shook his head. Words eluded him, and he realized he needed to sit down lest he fall. His knees unhinged; he found a chair and sat heavily.

"I find it terribly hard to believe that you would do such a thing and not tell us," his father continued. "You knew good and well that the Hershells promised Flora to you, and that it was an important, very important, word to keep. The dowry from Flora's *vadder* was the only way you'd have enough land and cows so you would have your own *haus*, and your own farm. What do you have to say for yourself?"

"I don't, I don't know what to say." And it was the truth. Abram's thoughts twisted upon one another so tightly that he feared for the worst. He looked at the girl, but she refused to look back at him. Why? He couldn't figure that out. She just sat there, shoulders shaking with silent sobs, while she wrung her hands in misery. Was she familiar? Maybe, maybe not. There had been a lot of dark-haired beauties he'd spent time with on *rumspringa*. Was she one of them?

His mother finally rose, but only to refill the girl's glass of water. His mother didn't look at him, and Abram didn't blame her.

"More to the point," his father said. "I don't know why you'd marry a girl and just leave her. Especially after you'd consummated the marriage. Why?"

"I don't really have anything to say about it. I already said that I don't know her."

"Normally, I'd be inclined to believe you." His father shifted a little, and approached the girl to put a comforting hand on her shoulder. "But she knew you. She has a marriage certificate and a photograph of the two of you immediately after you were married." His father pointed to a table under the window.

Abram looked at the items on the table, and said nothing. He sucked his teeth and looked away. His cheeks burned, and he clenched his hands together in a white-knuckled knot. His thoughts had turned into a riot of confusion and anger.

"Regardless of anything that has happened, the young lady needs help. And if you did do this, then you need to do right by her." The weight of his father's words sat heavily on his shoulders, and heavier still in the pit of his stomach. "Will you do right by this woman?" His father's judgmental gaze burned through him.

There was no acceptable way to answer that question. Abram groaned inwardly. Saying 'yes' would be a sign of admission; saying 'no' would be a quick way to be kicked out and ostracized. Neither option sat well with him.

"Will you do right by this woman?" His father's question was sharper than before. "Or will you leave her to suffer with this child on her own without a proper *vadder* for it? Will you condemn her to that fate?"

"I..., of course, *Dat*. Of course, I'll do right by her." It was a struggle to get the words out. He shot a fleeting look at Ida, and she shrank away with a fresh spate of silent tears.

His father leaned forward, elbows on his knees. He looked long and hard at both of them, his expression unreadable. Abram shifted uncomfortably under the weight of his father's stare, and found his hands quite interesting to look at. At some point, his mother left the room, leaving the three of them alone together.

"You'll be writing a letter to the Hershells explaining why you won't be taking Flora to be your *fraa*. We were planning on sending you off along with Matthew and Hannah, but the Hershells will have to make do with just Matthew and Hannah for now. If they'll even take them on as help." He pinched the bridge of his nose between his knuckles, and blew out a frustrated sound.

Mr. King's attention turned to Ida, who looked up with bleary eyes at him. "As you can see, we're not terribly well-off. We'll have a proper community wedding for the two of you soon, once we get all of this awfulness sorted. For now, you'll have to share a room with the girls until we can work something else out. There might be enough room in the hayloft for you, Abram, or you can bunk on the couch here. The girls have taken over your room." He looked up at Abram. "Ida tells us she's willing to join the community, and will be baptized after she takes the instructions."

Abram's hands were still incredibly interesting to him.

His father looked to the girl again. "You'll be expected to earn your keep, mind you. Even Abigail and Hannah, my son's wives work around this place. I'm not sure what kind of life he promised you, Ida, but this probably wasn't it."

"I understand," she murmured.

"Can you cook? Clean? What can you do that can be of service to all of us?"

She shifted a little and grimaced. "I can do all of that, Mr. King, sir. I can cook, clean and sew. I'm not so good at the sewing, but I can learn quickly to be better." Her mouth pulled to one side. "I grew up on a farm. We mostly had goats and cows, so I'm a fair hand with those. I can milk them, feed them..." she trailed off, and her breath hitched in her chest. "I'll do whatever you need me to, so long as... as..." Sobs broke her words apart.

Mr. King leaned forward, and pressed a comforting hand to her shoulder. "No need for that, now. You can call me Benjamin - or *Dat* if you'd rather."

She nodded, but no more words came.

Abram continued to study his hands, fingers tightly twisted together in a curious play of tendons and knuckles under his skin. He finally looked up when the talking stopped, and looked from his father to the girl.

Benjamin looked back at him, and his expression was a hard one. "As I said, the girls have your room now, so you'll be sleeping out here; I guess it'll be warmer than the hay loft. Go let your mother know to prepare the girls' room for another, understood?"

"*Jah*." Abram stood up.

"Not now," his father said.

Abram wanted to get out of the room. That was all that was on his mind.

"Ida, we'll have our community midwife come see you. I'm sorry this had to happen this way, but I hope you'll find we're good people, and we'll take care of you." Benjamin glared at his son some more.

Ida nodded, sniffed, and looked at her hands in a brief mirroring of Abram's posture.

Abram could only muster numbness over the whole thing. He felt as though he was in a bad dream. He looked at the girl out of the corner of his eye. Could she have made all this up, but for what purpose? Abram wanted to run away from the girl and his father. If he could get away by himself, he could think this thing through properly. All he had to wait for were his father's words of dismissal and he would be gone. Those words didn't come soon enough.

CHAPTER THREE

A merry heart doeth good like a medicine: but a broken
spirit drieth the bones.
Proverbs 17:22

Dinner was a tense affair. It was clear to Abram that everyone else had been told in private about the situation, and he wasn't sure if that was for the better. Sara and Edith fidgeted, and sent sidelong looks at Ida; his sisters-in-law were much less furtive about it. Even his brothers sat further away from him than usual, and his father didn't speak, save to give their traditional prayer.

It was only at the end of the meal that Benjamin, Abram's father, finally spoke.

"Abram and Ida will see to the dishes. Tomorrow, you'll see to Luke's duties as well as your own. Ida, you'll help in the house with Edith and Sara. We'll sort out what you're best at in due course." There was no room for discussion. Dishes had never been a job for a man in their household before. Abram guessed that his father only had him do dishes, so he and Ida would be forced to speak.

Abram's chin dipped in a half-nod.

Ida murmured a muted, "Yes, sir."

While his father took the rest of the family into the main room to read from the Bible, Abram and Ida retreated to the kitchen. The silence sat heavily on Abram's shoulders, and filled his stomach with a dead weight. Once in a while, Abram looked over at Ida, only to look away with a blush of shame.

The silence finally cracked under its own weight. Abram could feel her eyes on him, but he didn't turn to look. He didn't need to.

"I'm... I'm sorry," Ida said.

"Are you?" He made no effort to dilute the bitterness in his voice.

She recoiled as if struck. "I am, Abram. I truly am. I just, well what else was I to do? What else could I do?" She thrust out her ring-bearing hand. Light caught on the wedding band, and the tiny diamonds flickered. He reached out and caught her fingers, but only to cover the betraying diamonds and metal. "You gave this to me. You promised…"

"*Nee*, I'd never give you a ring. We Amish don't wear jewelry; it's vanity, for vain people. You'd better take it off if you're going to try to fit in around here." Abram shook his head vehemently. "This was a trick, this thing, all of it. You tricked me and now look. Look! My family doesn't trust me anymore. They might even trust you more than me." He clenched her hand and abruptly let go of it. "This is your fault. You shouldn't have come here."

"We're married now. You have to accept that."

"I have to accept the fact that you deceived me in the first place?" He gripped the edge of the counter, and shut his eyes. His shoulders bunched up, and he took a few deep breaths to try to calm down. "And now this?" He nodded his head toward her swollen belly. "Your condition?"

"It's a baby and I can't fake that," she replied flatly. "This is as real as it can get, and the child is yours. I didn't think you were so drunk you wouldn't remember our wedding night. Or, is that a convenient lie, so you won't feel the guilt of running away from me?"

"Is it mine?" Abram looked over his shoulder at her, and narrowed his eyes. "Because I'm pretty sure that's just another pretty little lie you're willing to tell anyone."

"It is yours, and we're married," she hissed. Tears formed in her eyes, and her hands balled into futile fists. "That night, that very night that we were married…"

"I was probably too drunk to do such a thing and you know it. It'd be a marvel if I were even awake after we shared vows, if we even did that properly."

The memory of the night was hazy at best. Abram struggled to pick through it, but the details were elusive. Still, he could not deny that he did have vague memories, even though he did not want to admit to having them. "Besides," he added with a sneer, "You look a lot bigger than you would be if that were the case. The child isn't mine at all, is it? Do you even know who the real father is?"

The tears in her eyes began to fall, fast and silent, while she bit her lower lip. "How dare you? How *dare* you?" She looked away and buried her face in her hands.

"You can't even look me in the eye to tell me, can you?" Abram released the counter and turned around, shoulders squared. Anger bubbled up through him and set his cheeks on fire. "You can't. Because you know the truth."

"You weren't this cruel when we met." Ida sobbed. "You were so nice and sweet, and you made so many promises…"

"And not once did I promise to marry you." That much he thought he remembered. He vaguely recalled she was a dancer and a girl full of laughter, but even in an inebriated state, he would have known better than to marry a girl like that. "I only remember a glimpse of you as a dancer in - in some-place that no wife of mine would ever go."

"You did though." She sniffed and finally looked at him. "You did marry me. There were witnesses."

"Witnesses to me being too drunk to know my name, sure. Witnesses who could attest that I was in no state to make any kind of decision greater than where I was going to pass out."

Her expression twisted. "Is that what you want me to tell your mother and father? That you were drunk when we were wed? Is that what you want me to tell our child?"

Abram's eyes narrowed, and his jaw clenched. But when the realization of what she'd said hit him, his eyes widened. "No. No, and you wouldn't dare."

"Wouldn't I?" She spat to one side. "I'm the one who tricked you into giving me a ring after all. Isn't that your story?" Ida wagged her fingers at him, making the light dance on the pesky piece of jewelry. "They already know that it was a proper wedding with witnesses and all. I just wonder what your father will say when he finds out you were blind drunk."

Abram lunged and caught her arm above the elbow. He pulled her in close and hissed, "You won't. I don't care that you would or that you can, but you will not do such a thing. I don't know who the father of your child is, but you're going to take that ring off. Then you're going to tell my parents that you lied, and you will leave and never come back to darken our doorstep ever again. Is that understood?"

"You're hurting me!" She struggled in his grip, eyes opened wide in terror. "Stop!"

The voices in the living room had dropped to a dull murmur, so Abram let her go. He said nothing further until the conversation in the other room had shifted back to normal, or close enough. He pressed in closer to her, all but pinning her to the wall. "Do you understand? That is what you're going to do. What you have to do, otherwise my life will be ruined."

Tears welled in her eyes again. "Don't you understand? Don't you have a heart? I didn't have any other choice, Abram. I just... I didn't." This time, her tears flowed. Her eyes met his, and she didn't try to escape. "My father won't have me in his house. My mother won't talk to me. My sisters and brother have disowned me, they all think I'm an unwed mother. They won't believe I'm married, because you're not around. What else could I do? I had to come here. I had to come to you."

"But why? Why me?" Anger and bewilderment colored Abram's voice, and he forced himself to step back and away. "Why? What did I do to you? Why do I deserve this?"

"I already told you why," she said. Her voice was soft. "You were nice, sweet. You talked to me. You were the only good one there. And I- it just…" Her knees buckled, and she began to slide down the wall. Abram hastened to catch her and managed to snare her under the arms. She flung her arms around his neck, and buried her face in his chest.

The feeling of her swollen stomach against him was unsettling. While she sobbed, shoulders heaving and body trembling, he rested his chin on the top of her head and stroked her back. He stared at the blank wall in front of his face while his mind raced.

He couldn't pull up any more memories from that time. The whole year he's spent on *rumspinga* he was working as a laborer, and when he wasn't working, he'd been in a liquor-induced haze.

Abram made a mental note to talk to Harry about it later. Maybe he would remember more, but he wasn't about to hold his breath on it. Still, it was worth a shot. His thoughts turned again to the young woman in his arms. There was no denying that situation, not entirely. Even if she did tell his parents, and they deemed the wedding invalid, he would have to suffer from his father's judgment for a long time - maybe even forever.

But would that be better than this? Suffering through a marriage with a woman he barely knew? A woman pregnant with a child that most likely wasn't his? He grimaced. She stirred against him and he loosened his grip, but all she sought to do was look up at him.

"Please. Please, just… help me for now. Help me until the baby's born. After that, after that, I promise I'll leave." She sucked her lower lip in, and looked up at him with bright green eyes that still swam with tears. "I just, I really need help, and I don't have anyone else I can turn to. Not anymore."

The sight of her distress wrenched every last one of his heartstrings. The last of his anger bled away, and he blew out a breath. Abram shut his eyes for a long moment to let his thoughts sort themselves out. In the end, he said, "Only until the child is born, is that clear? I'll not have you break a promise on top of everything else." He quickly figured that when she left after the baby was born, he would say that she ran away - they could hardly hold him accountable for that.

A flash of frustration and anger cut across her features, but it was quickly overwhelmed with gratitude. She hugged him fiercely, and he returned it, though not nearly so fervently.

"Is everything alright in here?" Ruth poked her head in, concern creasing her forehead. "I heard crying. You didn't do anything to upset her, did you, Abram?"

Abram released his grip on Ida and jumped away from her. "*Nee, Mamm*. Everything's fine. We were just speaking loudly." Abram forced a fake smile for his mother. "Though I should go to bed soon. Long day tomorrow, for both of us." Abram looked back at Ida and she nodded. He could hear his mother in the doorway, and imagined she must have been wringing her hands.

"It'll be a longer day yet for your *vadder* and Luke," Ruth said after a moment. "They'll be planning out the best place to put the pair of you. And once the baby comes…" she trailed off and clicked her tongue. "Well, I suppose we'll have to talk to your *familye* at some point, Ida."

"I know," Ida said, but her words were muffled. She turned her head in Ruth's direction. "I know. It's just that it's not the right time right now. They've had a hard time of it."

"I can only imagine," Ruth said with a heavy sigh. "Come on, then. We have a cot for you in the girls' room. Abram, there should be plenty in the main room for you - blankets and the like. Let's get the lot of you squared away, hmm?"

"Yes, ma'am," Ida said.

"Go on, then." Abram stepped back toward the kitchen sink.

It was only after they were gone that he went to his temporary room, the living room. Sleep was elusive and chased off by the rabid dogs that his thoughts had become. 'No rest for the wicked,' his father was fond of saying - and Abram finally fell asleep wondering if he was truly wicked.

CHAPTER FOUR

Blessed is the man that walketh not in the counsel of the
ungodly, nor standeth in the way of sinners,
nor sitteth in the seat of the scornful.
But his delight is in the law of the LORD;
and in his law doth he meditate day and night.

Psalms 1:1-2

*A*s Ida rested in a chair at the kitchen table, she peered out the window at a majestic oak that had caught her eye, while contemplating her situation. She was grateful to Abram's family for giving them a cottage to stay in on the edge of their farm. She wondered if coming to find Abram had been a mistake. If it were best for the baby, she would endure Abram's hostility.

She was adamant that her baby would grow up with his or her father. She remembered the expression on the faces of Abram's parents when she told them that the baby was Abram's. It was a mixture of shock, disapproval, and disgust. She knew that they were very religious, so their look was justified, but they could have been a little nicer to her considering she was carrying their grandchild. Ever since Ida had said that that the baby was Abram's, she'd felt an overwhelming sense of alienation. Her own family had disowned her, and Abram's family merely tolerated her out of necessity, or out of a sense of moralistic duty.

Seeing that she was not wanted in that house, Ida understood that there was no point in trying to make Abram change his mind regarding her and the baby. She hoped she might be able to change Abram. Every woman's hope was to change the man she had alongside her, making him change according to her likings, or so Ida had thought. She believed that with time Abram would understand that he had a responsibility towards the baby, even if he felt nothing for her.

Every day there was tension. Ida was trying her best to be a good and loving wife, but she knew that Abram was just there going through the motions. In his heart, he didn't see it as a real marriage.

There was no real love in his heart for her, Ida was certain of that. He had finally admitted that he remembered meeting her once or twice when he was way over the limit of alcoholic consumption. Abram never admitted to or acknowledged the fact that they had gotten married. But, she was there living with him, so he had to have some knowledge or memory of his marriage, even if he never said so.

After she had come to search for Abram, Ida had in mind that she would endure everything that fate might bring into her path for the sake of having a husband and a father for her child. After she had lived with Abram for several weeks, she realized that life for a man was not easy, but life for a woman was much harder.

Ida decided she could stay and play the part of a wife who was loved, or she could go somewhere else and be true to herself. Even though a single woman with a child would be looked down upon, it couldn't make her feel any worse than she did living with Abram and his coldness toward her.

Abram was away for the day visiting his parents. It was a Sunday, and seeing it was the second Sunday without gatherings, it was a day when folk visited one another. Abram had not asked her if she wanted to visit anyone, or if she wanted to accompany him. She was left alone, while Abram had taken their only buggy, forcing her to stay at home. This was not how Ida had pictured her marriage. He had no regard for her or her feelings.

She waited until she was certain her husband was at a safe distance before she packed her things. Everything she owned fit into a small suitcase. The suitcase was quite wonky, and looked as though it had been well used. It could have been the suitcase Abram had used on his *rumspringa.* Ida stared at the sad suitcase, and considered that it resembled her life perfectly - hopeless and barely holding together.

Ida was in pain and her belly was full of unrest. Probably the baby felt her state of mind and was agitated, but nothing could stop Ida from leaving. She was determined to disappear from that place; she wanted to forget about Abram and everything related to him. She would have to start off on foot, and she hoped that she'd be able to flag someone down and get a ride into town. They lived a safe distance from the 'temptations' of the town, which was what Abram's father liked to call them, since he was a strictly religious man. The word of God was everything to the King family.

She looked around the small farmhouse that she had tried to make a home. All her efforts had gone unnoticed and unappreciated by Abram. The atmosphere was cold and barren, reflecting Abram's heart toward her. Ida slammed the door behind her, ready to make a new life for herself and her child. She crossed the road and walked beside it, heading to town.

She was glad at least that Abram had stopped telling her that he wanted her to go. He never mentioned that she would have to leave as soon as the baby was born. It was only that first night in his parents' house that he'd told her she'd have to leave after the baby was born. She wondered if Abram had any feelings for her at all. She had loved him when she married him. Ida had been drawn to Abram at first, but he had been a different Abram. He wasn't the moody and sullen man that he was now.

If it weren't for Abram's parents, Ida knew that she and Abram wouldn't have spent the last several weeks in the small house that they'd shared. They weren't living as man and wife - their separate bedrooms attested to that. Abram insisted on sleeping in the tiny second bedroom. Either he didn't want to be married at all, or he was determined to keep her as far away as possible.

She turned and looked back at the small house. Ida wrapped her shawl around her shoulders to keep out a chilly wind that swept across her. Turning back to the direction of town, she hoped a wagon or buggy would come along soon. She didn't want to walk past Abram's parents' house, which was between her and town. After a few paces, she heard hoof beats and turned to see her neighbor, Patrick, approaching in his wagon. She waved him down.

"Heeeyy haaa!!" he yelled to his two large, brown horses. They stopped at his command. "What are you doing here in the middle of the road alone?"

"Hey Patrick, would you mind taking me to town? Abram's got the buggy, and I just remembered I have an errand to run, and it won't wait until tomorrow." Ida fought back tears. She didn't want to be in the constant position of asking favors of everyone. It wasn't believable that she had an errand to run on a Sunday, and she hoped he wouldn't pry.

"I can take you into town. Jump in." Patrick jumped down from the wagon. "I'll help you up."

Ida smiled, glad for his help. With one hand under her arm, Patrick guided Ida up into the wagon, and then put her suitcase in the back. "Thank you, Patrick."

Once Patrick jumped back into his wagon, he asked, "Where you off to by yourself? Going somewhere, without your husband? Why isn't Abram taking you into town? I saw him passing in his buggy not ten, or twenty minutes ago."

"It's a long story. I have to get into town, and he had to see his parents. I have some things to resolve."

Patrick nodded, and Ida was glad that he asked nothing further.

Once Ida got into town, she had no idea where to go, because she had only been to the town twice since she'd been living with Abram.

She knew no one and had no idea what to do. Everyone gave her strange looks, and everything seemed hard and unsettling. *What am I going to do now?* She knew she wouldn't go back to the little house and live with Abram in silence. Anything had to be better than his silent disapproval.

Ida saw a church building across the street, and wondered if they might help her. She pushed the door open, but there was no priest, or minister, just a woman cleaning the place. Maybe the lady might be able to help her, or know where she could go. "Good day, dear lady. I'm here looking for shelter. I am an expectant woman all alone, and I don't know the town too well."

The woman straightened her back, and looked Ida up and down. "What's your name?"

"Ida, madam, my name is Ida!"

"Ida, you can't stay in the church, but I know a refuge for poor and troubled people where you can stay for a while, until you sort things out. You are looking for a place to stay?"

Ida smiled glad that she had a possible place to stay. "Yes, I am."

The old lady continued, "No one will ask a dime from you, so you can rest assured that no one will throw you out of there."

"Thank you very much," Ida said, trying to find a

place or a stair where she could sit. Her back was hurting her from the bumpy ride in the wagon.

"I can take you there when I finish up here, if you'd care to wait."

"Yes, I can wait, thank you."

"I must warn you that the conditions you'll find in there will not be good. But we're trying to make them better for people." The woman grabbed the broom as if she were going to start to use it.

"Don't worry, ma'am, I'm used to hard conditions, thank you again." Ida sat down and waited for the woman to finish.

As she sat, many thoughts crossed her mind. She tried to come up with a plan that would save both her and the child. How would she ever live a good life with no money? Before marrying Abram, she was a dancer in a dance hall. Ida's parents had disowned her the first time for working in the dance hall, they had told her no good would come of working in a place like that. It was no surprise that they hadn't changed their minds about her when she told them she was expecting a child, and was jilted by her husband. Ida had made good friends when she was a dancer, and she wondered if one of her friends might take her in for a time.

THE SHELTER WAS ONLY a couple of streets away from the church. When they got there, Ida could see only a broken cottage with a broken window. A dozen people were sitting outside the place looking destitute.

Ida swallowed hard. The night was going to be a cold one, so at least she'd have a roof over her head and some warmth. But, she could not stay in that place longer than one night. The kind lady from the church showed her over the house that was used as a shelter. There were no private rooms; beds were edge to edge across every room, except for the kitchen and bathrooms. Belongings were tucked under beds.

Ida was shown to a bed in the corner of one room. Before she stowed her bag under her bed, she tucked some money that she'd taken from the house into the front of her dress. The money was equivalent to two weeks' worth of food. She knew that Abram would not suffer the loss of the money because he had food from the farm, and he could always eat at his parents' or his brother's house.

The old lady then led her outside, and toward a man who appeared to be in his early thirties.

The old lady said, "James, this is, Ida."

The man, who was either vague or hard of hearing, leaned forward and said, "What's your name?"

"My name is Ida."

"My name is Earl, by the way."

"Earl knows the place, so I'll leave you with him," the old lady said.

"Thank you very much, I appreciate your help." Ida smiled at the lady, and when the lady walked away, Ida felt alone. She hoped she'd done the right thing by leaving Abram. Earl patted the chair next to him, and she sat down.

"So, what brings you to this old shack, Ida?" asked Earl.

Ida took a deep breath, glad to have someone to talk to. "Months ago, I was working in a dance hall and this man named Abram came walking in. He was a very nice and polite man, and handsome. He'd obviously had a little too much to drink that night, seeing how he stumbled in. Even when he was drunk, he was well mannered. After my shift ended, he rushed to talk to me, and said that he wanted to marry me. I just laughed it off and went home.

"Go on."

"He was back the next night, and the next. It went on every night for months, and I grew fond of him. We'd talk for hours some nights. I don't know what came over me, but one night I said 'yes,' I would marry him. There was a judge who married everyone, and we went to him, he married us and his wife took a photo, and she was our witness."

"Next morning, Abram was gone. So I found out where he lived from the man he was staying with, and came and found him to get him to help with the child. His family is very religious and not very accepting of the situation. It's a huge mess." Ida sniffed back her tears. "I don't know what to do now."

Earl said, "So your baby's a bastard?"

"No, don't say that. We were married," Ida said, wondering why she was telling a stranger her sad tale.

"Well, since you told your story, you might as well hear my story. About a year ago, I ran a successful saloon, and got married to the prettiest girl in town. She had locks of gold that matched the beams of the sun, and beautiful eyes that reminded me of the ocean. She was nice at first, but later turned into a shrew. One night we got into a huge fight about something that I said. Then, after I fell asleep that night, she burned down my saloon, then she stole all my money and rode off with my favorite horse, leaving me broke and without my business. So I found this place, and have been living here ever since."

"I'm sorry that happened to you," Ida said, wondering whose situation was worse.

"Well, I get by," Earl replied.

Another man sat next to Ida and said, "Hello."

"Ida, this is Tex."

"Hello, Tex."

"Tell 'er why you're here, Tex," Earl said.

Tex laughed heartily. "To think a year ago I was one of the richest men around, and now I'm sitting here with an old man and some floozy."

"That's rude," Ida said, and stood up.

Tex grabbed her arm. "I'm sorry, don't go. I've lost my manners along with all my money, and dignity, it seems."

Ida sat back down. She had nowhere else to be.

"You wanna hear my story?"

"I don't, but you may as well tell the lady," Earl said.

"The lady hasn't heard my story," the man said. "I'll start again." He glared at Earl, and then looked at Ida and clicked his tongue. "I'm Tex."

"Hello again, Tex."

Tex pulled his chair closer. "So anyways, I was a cowboy a year ago, my men and I were the best around, and I lived near Texas. If you had any cattle that ran away, we were the ones that you got to go get 'em back. We caught the cattle of those big money ranchers. So one day we got a job from Thomas Finch. His best cattle got out, so he said he was going to pay the most money we'd ever seen. So we went out to get 'em. After about five hours on their trail, we finally found them and started to herd 'em back home. Then one of my men drew a gun and shot over my horse's head, sending him charging into the desert. He finally bucked me off, leaving me stranded in the desert without nuthin' but the clothes on my back, and my dried leather canteen. I passed out and woke up in a hospital. Couldn't remember nuthin' for days. Now I have nuthin' and nowhere to live 'cept this place. Here, I can get a warm meal and a place to sleep."

Ida asked, "Why would your men betray you like that, and how did you get here?"

"Some people have no rules, and they will do anything to make some extra money. I don't know how I ended up here, but one place is as good as another when you ain't got no family," Tex said.

Ida knew exactly what Tex meant about having no family. Abram's family came with conditions, and her family had disowned her. She wondered if anyone cared what happened to her.

THAT NIGHT IN THE SHELTER, Ida could not sleep. She was comforted a little by the sounds of the heavy rain that fell from the sky, glad that she had a roof over her head.

People, lost people who had no future and no will to change their current situation, surrounded her. Wherever she looked, she would see people who were blaming either God, fate or someone else for what had happened to them. Ida wondered if they'd ever get away from their circumstances. She knew that she would have to do just that for the sake of the baby. She could not give up like these people had.

Lying there listening to the rain, she thought over her options. She struggled to keep her attention on positive thoughts rather than the negative ones that were crowding in on her, such as little money, no home, and no father for her baby.

If she could stay somewhere until the baby was born, she could return to her dancing job. She'd thought a lot about God during her stay with the King family. She had been baptized and taken the instructions. Under the circumstances of her fast arrival into the community, and her unexpected marriage to Abram, the bishop had taken her through the teachings at a fast pace. She had believed in God before her stay in the community, but her belief had been in her head and not in her heart, as it was now.

God forgive me for turning back to my old lifestyle of dancing in a worldly place, but what else am I to do?

Please show me how I can take care of the baby and myself and live a life that you would have me live. Ida closed her eyes and was able to have a little sleep.

That next morning, she gathered her things and set off for the train station. It was a long and cold walk, but soon she had bought her ticket, and was seated waiting for the train. Her old friends in Virginia were nearly a day's train ride away. She saw going back to Virginia, as her only hope for a decent future.

Fearful thoughts were never far from her mind. When she had lived in Virginia, she had lived with a friend, but she'd paid a monthly rent that she could not afford this time. She understood a long time ago that friends are friends only up to a point when money is involved.

CHAPTER FIVE

And ye now therefore have sorrow: but I will see you
again, and your heart shall rejoice,
and your joy no man taketh from you.
John 16:22

~ The Day Before ~

*A*bram knew that his parents were very strict, and from being on his *rumspringa,* he knew just how conservative the Amish community was. His family was the most important thing to him, and that was the same with the whole community; family and community were first, and they supported each other as one large family.

Abram's father had always told him that they were to

bear each other's burdens. When he'd visited his father, he'd been reminded of the Scripture in 1 Timothy, *But if any provide not for his own, and especially for those of his own house, he hath denied the faith, and is worse than an infidel.* His father had always said that, 'We should endure the way Lord Jesus endured.'

On the way back home, he knew he'd been horrible to Ida. Ida was sweet to him and did everything that a proper wife should. He would ask her to forgive him for how he'd been treating her.

Forgive me Gott for how I've treated Ida. I will be a proper husband to her as she's been a proper fraa to me. I will tell Ida I'll always be there to care for her and the boppli.

He knew that it didn't matter whether the baby was his or not. She had proof that he had married her, and he had to stand by that.

A feeling of peace flowed over him. He knew that his life would be happy from this point on. He was doing the right thing and putting selfishness behind him. He sang a hymn as his horse clip clopped toward his small home. When his house came into view, his heart was gladdened, and for the first time he was looking forward to seeing his wife. Ida would be anxiously waiting for him with a cup of coffee and a bright smile. He knew that Ida would be delighted with his change of heart.

He pulled up his horse in front of the barn, and after he unhitched the buggy, he tended to the horse and put him in his stall. With a huge smile, he hurried toward the house, anxious to ask forgiveness of his new wife.

"Ida, Ida!" Abram called out. When he saw she wasn't waiting for him as usual, he went through the house calling her name. He checked every room, but she wasn't there.

Abram flung himself onto the couch and rubbed his face with both hands. She was gone, and it served him right. He'd treated her dreadfully. He sprang to his feet, hoping she'd just gone for a walk in the woods. Abram stepped outside, and walked a little way from the house calling out to her. After ten minutes, he became worried. She had to have gone somewhere on foot, since they only had one horse and buggy.

He walked the half-mile to his nearest neighbor's house to see if they had heard or seen something of Ida. Before he reached the house, he saw his neighbor, Patrick, driving his wagon on a nearby road. Abram sprinted to the road and reached Patrick's horses.

Abram jumped right in front of the horses, forcing Patrick to pull them to an urgent halt.

"Are you crazy or what?" Patrick jumped down from his wagon, and walked straight to Abram. "You want to get yourself killed or something, Abram?" He grabbed Abram by his shirt pulling him toward him. He let go of Abram's shirt when he looked into his face. "What's wrong; what's happened?" Patrick asked.

Abram stood in silence, shaking his head, searching for words. His neighbor Patrick was an *Englischer*, and now Abram had to tell him that his wife had run away from him. It was hardly a good example for him to set. He only had himself to blame. He hung his head in silent shame.

"C'mon, man, just tell me what happened. Are you just gonna stand there like a chicken, or what? Speak."

Abram choked back tears. "I can't find Ida."

"You can't what?" Patrick asked.

"I can't find Ida. She's not at home. It's as if she disappeared into the air."

"She didn't come back yet?"

"What did you say?" Abram asked, hoping that Patrick knew something.

"I took her into town earlier today because she told me she had some business there, and you were at your parents. She was walking there with a suitcase, so I offered to drive her."

"You took Ida to town, with a suitcase? When?"

"Well, I'm nearly certain it was past midday, around 2 p.m. I think."

Patrick leaned forward, and with a smile said, "Trouble in paradise?"

Abram stepped back. "Did she say where she was going?"

Patrick scratched his head. "I can't recall, and that's the truth of it."

"Did you take her to the train station?"

"No, not close to the station. I'm sorry, Abram, I had no idea what was happening."

"The suitcase, and her walking on her own didn't give you a clue?" Abram spat out.

"Hey, Abram, it's not for me to look after your household. Better to look to yourself. Where were you?"

Abram scratched his head. "Thanks for the information, and I'm sorry for scaring your horses."

Patrick did not reply. Abram walked away angry, with himself that he'd been so awful to Ida that she'd left him without a word. Abram walked back to his house wondering what to do. He'd have to find her. As soon as he got back home, he pulled on his coat, hitched the buggy and drove into town.

It was getting dark when he arrived. Abram tied his buggy and went into one of the two saloons that were open. They would surely remember an expectant woman dressed in plain clothing. The first one was full of drunken men waving pistols around in the air and hollering. Abram couldn't see any women in the saloon, let alone his woman. Places like that left him cold now, but only a few months ago he'd been one of the rowdy mob. He was glad he'd chosen to return to his community.

When he walked into the second saloon, an old man,

who could barely walk from drunkenness, bumped into him.

"Hey, old man, did you see an expectant woman in the last few hours, looking for shelter or something?"

The old man looked up at Abram. "I ain't seen nuthin' of the kind But, if she isn't from here and has no money on her, she'll probably be at the shelter. If she's got money, she'll be at the hotel - who knows." The man stumbled further into the saloon.

Abram didn't know of any shelter. He walked through the town the whole night. When it rained, he went back to his buggy and pulled on his coat. He knocked on every place that lodged people, but still there was no sign of her. He staggered back to the buggy to get a couple of hours sleep. He would start looking again at first light.

When the sky had lifted above the horizon the next morning, Abram opened his eyes. He realized where he was, and jumped down from his buggy determined to find her. He saw the train station not far, so went to look at the timetable thinking she might intend to return to Virginia.

He walked into the train station, and the first person

he saw was Ida. She was sitting alone and looked very cold. His heart was glad, and all he wanted to do was hold her in his arms.

IDA LOOKED up and saw Abram walking toward her. She didn't know whether to be happy or fearful. She'd run away from him for a reason. The man heading toward her with open arms seemed a totally changed man. She wondered whether he was putting on an act for others to see, or maybe his parents had made him come to find her.

"I'm taking you home," he said, as he put his arm around her, and heaved her to her feet. "Forgive me for how I've been to you. I don't want to lose you. Will you come home with me?"

Ida looked into his eyes. Maybe this was an answer to her prayers. It seemed right for her to be with the father of her baby. Maybe he was hoping for another chance; maybe he'd be better. He truly seemed pleased to see her. She didn't know what to do. All she knew was that she didn't want things to be as they were before.

"Are you coming? Look, Ida, I'm truly sorry," he

whispered. "I need to talk to you and tell you how I've changed, but I don't want to do it here." Abram looked around the station.

Ida nodded. "I'll come with you."

Abram leaned down and grabbed her suitcase. "Let's go."

CHAPTER SIX

Be careful for nothing; but in every thing by prayer and
supplication with thanksgiving
let your requests be made known unto God.
Philippians 4:6

*E*ven if Ida didn't believe things were going
to get better as weeks passed, she observed
that Abram's behavior had changed. He was no
longer silent and moody. Now, he was respectful to
her. She'd come back hoping that he was going to
change fully and be a proper husband to her.

Abram had improved greatly, but still, Ida did not
feel that he loved her as a man should love a woman.

He was polite, and it seemed as though he was nice because he had to be nice, and not because he wanted to be nice from his heart.

"Why are you treating me like this?" Ida asked, when Abram was painting their living room.

"What happened, dear?" Abram asked, placing his painting brush down. "What have I done to upset you?"

"Why are you treating me as if I were your *schweschder*? Why won't you look at me properly; why don't you look at me like a man would look at his woman? What is wrong with me?"

"I don't understand." Abram frowned.

"That is the problem; you don't understand that I love you. Why can't you love me back? Why can't you show me some of those feelings buried deep down in your heart? Do you have a heart, at least, or it is made of ice?" Ida folded her arms across her chest.

Abram shrugged his shoulders after a moment of silence. "I'm trying to be a *gut* husband. I'm told love grows; I'm doing my best."

Ida turned around and walked back into the kitchen.

There it was; she had her answer. Abram did not love her. She wanted someone to love her, not just to have a pretend marriage and live together as husband and wife for the outside world to see. She'd given up a lot for him and what had he given up for her?

Ida marched back into the living room. "Abram King, I've changed my religion for you, I've become Amish, I've gotten baptized, and I'm learning Pennsylvania Dutch as fast as I can. I've changed my whole life for you and for the baby. And what have you done? You don't even love me." Ida felt tears coming to her eyes, as she realized the situation was useless. Angry words were not going to cause Abram to love her. Angry words would only drive him further from her. She could not do anything to make him love her.

"I don't know what to say, Ida. I don't know what you want me to say. I'm here aren't I? I'm looking after you, and I'll be here to look after the *boppli* too."

Ida walked up the stairs to her bedroom. They had separate rooms, which proved to Ida their marriage was a sham. Yes, he was nice to her and provided for her, but that's not how she had pictured their marriage. It was clear that he was never going to love her, and she was not going to stay in a loveless marriage. She had to leave him, but she had to be smarter about it this time. She wouldn't leave him until she had a proper plan of escape.

She started writing letters to all the friends she'd ever had to ask about the possibility of a place to stay until after the baby was born. Then she would find a way to take care of the baby and herself.

The next day, she asked Abram to take her to town to get some supplies. It was then that she posted all her letters. She put a lot of hope in those letters, because they were her last chance to freedom, her last chance to grasp at least a little happiness in life.

Two weeks had passed and finally she received a response from one of her good friends, Millie. Millie was a lady who Ida had worked for when she had first started dancing.

After reading it, Ida hid the letter from Abram's sight, because she was afraid he would stop her from going. Millie had said that she could go anytime she wanted, and Millie was getting a room ready for her. Ida recalled Millie had a large apartment over the saloon. Ida was grateful for somewhere to go, and decided to go as soon as possible. If the opportunity came up, she would go the very next day.

She went to sleep that night with her head packed with ideas and scenarios, and she couldn't stop thinking of how things were going to turn out after she had left him. She loved Abram, but what use was that if he didn't love her back?

Ida had gotten up early every morning to prepare Abram a cooked breakfast, and the next morning, on her day of escape to Virginia, was no different. After breakfast, Ida heard the clip clop of Abram's buggy heading away from the house. She'd already packed her small suitcase, and she headed up the stairs to fetch it. She took money out of the cookie jar. It wasn't much, but it would get her a ticket to Virginia, and keep her in food for the next few weeks.

She picked up pen and paper from one of the kitchen drawers and wrote a note for Abram. She didn't want him to worry as he'd done last time she'd left him.

"DEAR ABRAM,

I decided to leave because I simply can't breathe in this house. I can't live in a place where I'm neither wanted nor loved. I simply can't function. I hope we would meet some other time under better circumstances, and who knows, maybe things will be different, and we would look at each other differently!

I will write to you when I get to where I'm going.

With love, your wife,

Ida."

IDA READ through the note and then she placed it on their kitchen table. She took one last look around the house. She wasn't sad to leave it, as the house held no happy memories. Ida took one last look over it only so she could remember the place where she had tried to make things work with her baby's father. She picked up her small suitcase, walked through the door and closed it behind her.

AFTER A LONG MORNING working on his parents' farm, instead of joining his family for the midday meal, Abram decided to go back to the house to show Ida the surprise he'd been working on. He'd been working on a crib for the baby, and had hidden it in the barn under a blanket in the corner.

He pulled up the buggy between the barn and the house. Abram jumped from the buggy, hurried to the barn, flung the blanket off the crib and carried it to the door of the house. Eventually, he'd paint the crib white, unless Ida wanted it varnished just the way it was. He pushed the door open and called Ida's name. There was no answer, so Abram placed the crib on the floor and went from room to room to look for her.

After a while, he found a note. After reading it a couple of times he still couldn't believe that she had left again without saying a word. He had been a good husband and had given her everything that she could have wanted. He'd given her a place to live, and they were planning a good future for their baby.

CHAPTER SEVEN

Casting all your care upon him;
for he careth for you.
1 Peter 5:7

The coach accommodations would do. They would have to do; they were all she could afford. With the money she'd taken from Abram, she needed to be as frugal as possible. *It has to last awhile,* she thought. *Taken* - that made what she'd done sound so criminal. She was no thief, and she knew it. *I only took what I would need. Besides, it's not for me, it's for the baby, our baby.*

The train would leave the station soon. Ida sat in her seat and waited hoping that no travelers would sit next to her. The last thing she wanted to do was talk to someone. She pursed her lips into a fixed expression, to discourage anyone who might sit alongside from mistaking her for a friendly woman eager for conversation. Looking at the empty seat next to her, she wondered how long it would stay empty. Some extra space would be luxury on this day-long journey.

A whistle blew indicating the train was about to depart. Moments later, she felt the shake and shimmy of the train moving on the rails. And that was when the first teardrops of the trip began to fall. She wiped at them frantically, willing them to stop. She didn't want to fall apart, not like this, not in such a public place. But they wouldn't stop, and she dripped like a leaky waterspout from Abram's small town through the next couple of stations.

A lace handkerchief waved gently in front of her face, and she looked in the direction of the hand holding it. So consumed with her own emotions that she hadn't noticed the seat next to her had been taken.

"Here, my dear. Do take this. Dry your eyes, child." The voice of the tiny woman who sat there, wearing a serviceable, simple, wool traveling dress, wasn't unkind. It was somehow comforting, in fact.

Ida took the offered handkerchief and began dabbing at her eyes. She managed to squeak out a 'thank you' through the sobs that wouldn't quit, and even gave a small smile to ensure the woman knew she was grateful.

"I don't mean to pry, but I've raised ten children, and I know how the tears come when those babies start growing in your belly," the woman said. "Seems to me I was a sniffling mess myself every single day I carried those babies inside me. Then, when they're born, they keep making you cry for the rest of your life, for one reason or another - they don't let you sleep, so you cry; they go off and leave you when they're older, so you cry; they die too young, and you cry then too. Babies and tears are a right normal partnership, in my experience."

"Makes me wonder why they're even worth it then," Ida said. "All these tears and all the worrying and wondering. Doesn't really seem worth all the trouble."

The woman chuckled softly, smiled, and reached over and patted Ida's hand. "Oh, they're worth it, you'll see. They bring the greatest joy you'll ever know on God's green earth, child; I promise you that. I take it this is your first then?"

"Yes, my first."

"And no one traveling with you, in your condition?"

"No," Ida replied. "I'm all alone." She thought about how alone she was in the world, and knew in her heart she wasn't just alone on this train - she was alone in life. With the exception of her friend, Millie, who was waiting for her on the other end of the trip, she only had a handful of people she knew.

Millie was a nice lady, but she wasn't family. Millie had given Ida her first dancing job at sixteen in the saloon she owned. And when the baby was born, she'd give her another job dancing, but she was just a friend, not family. Ida struggled with her new faith. Dancing was not permitted according to the *Ordnung*, and neither was mixing with unbelievers, the *Englischers*, but what else was she to do?

Would *Gott* have her live with a man who was forced to be with her, with no love in his heart? Maybe that's what *Gott* would want, but Ida knew she would be miserable living like that. Maybe she was just as bad a Christian as she'd been a wife. Maybe she should go back and suffer a loveless life with Abram if that's what God wanted.

The old woman started speaking again, causing Ida to jerk up her head.

"Well, I hope you've at least got your man or some kin folk waiting for you at the end of this train ride. Mamas-to-be need a lot of caring for; seems like you need some care yourself."

Ida realized then that she had a choice to make. She could either make up a tale about the wonderful, handsome husband waiting for her at her destination, or she could tell the truth and risk having to bear the older woman's disapproval.

She looked down at her belly, growing bigger every day. She patted her hand against it, wondering about the tiny babe inside. In that moment, she knew that the baby was changing her life already. Even in little things, like what to tell an old woman on a train. Ida knew she had a new, grand responsibility to this little babe. She had to live by example now, be the kind of woman she'd want this baby to respect and be able to learn from. Though she'd not yet gazed upon the soft, pink cheeks of her newborn, she was already a mother to her baby. What would she advise her own daughter to do in a situation like this?

She realized the old dear was still waiting for an answer. Ida looked at her, and said, "I have no one, ma'am. I have a friend, Millie, waiting for me. She's going to give me a place to stay while I care for this baby, and then she has work for me afterwards, once the baby's born."

"Oh, dear. I am so sad to hear it, child."

"It's okay, I'm strong, and I'll get by," Ida said, trying to convince herself of her own strength, probably more than she was trying to convince the woman.

"And the baby's father is…? Oh, I shouldn't pry. Forgive me."

"No, it's okay. I don't mind. The baby's father didn't want us," Ida said, but as she said it, she realized it didn't sound quite true. "Actually, I don't know if that's true. I know he isn't sure if he wants us, the baby and I, and I guess, I didn't really give him a chance to find out. I left."

"Oh, I see."

The two women were quiet for a time, both lost in their own thoughts, and taking long looks out the dusty train windows.

"I don't have all the answers, child. No one does. If someone tells you they know all the answers, they're probably selling something." The woman chuckled to herself. "But there is one thing I've learned to be true. At least, it was true for my William and I. Babies change everything. They make solid-thinking folks question the very ground they're standing on. They make folks do strange things, act strange ways, grow uncertain about whether they know up from down anymore."

"Again, I wonder why babies are even worth it," Ida said, smiling through the tears that had begun to fall again. "Babies sure do seem to create a lot of trouble in this world."

"There is one thing that babies do really well, better than any other creature on God's green earth." The older woman paused then, as if making a way through silence for the introduction of a big revelation. "They grow love. They grow it in places you didn't ever think it could grow. They grow it in ways

75

you'd never expect it should grow. They're like heavenly, little, angelic weeds, spreading love and bringing smiles to faces that never knew they could even feel love so deeply. Give it time, child. This man of yours, if he is anything like my William, he doesn't even know what a baby means. He's more scared than you are, and he's more confused than you are too. Your business is your own and you don't need to take the advice of a woman on a train, but do try one thing, child. Will you try one thing for me?"

Ida nodded, taking in the woman's kindness and advice like she would a tall glass of water on a lonely stretch of desert.

"Let him try. Don't turn him away. Give him some time to experience the magic of a baby. He might very well surprise you and become a man who is better, stronger and more loving than any man you could ever have imagined for yourself."

"Well, I guess he is trying," Ida said. "He has been trying to make me happy, in his own way. I guess that's something, isn't it?"

The woman laughed. "Well, yes, it's something."

Ida thought about the woman's words, turning them over and over in her mind. She thought of Abram then, of the little things they'd had together in the last few weeks. She thought of the bouquet of fresh daisies he'd surprised her with when she'd opened her eyes just yesterday morning. She thought of the shy way he'd asked her what she thought about naming the baby 'Abram,' if it were a boy, while he brought her a hot cup of tea after the evening meal.

The hours on the train flew by. So lost in her own thoughts was Ida that she barely recognized their passing. When the train pulled into the station, she caught a glimpse of Millie at the landing, waiting for her with a huge smile on her face.

It was a warm and welcoming smile and one that should have warmed her through to her very core. But she couldn't help wish that it was Abram waiting for her, and she was surprised to realize that the train ride had changed her. No longer was she angrily pursuing an escape from Abram. Now she wished she were running towards him, to work through the magic of this baby in whatever way they could, together. Still, she had made her decision and silly daydreams and hopeful ideas were not reality. Reality was that she would have to look after herself and her baby.

She stood to leave her seat and turned to hug the

older woman goodbye, but the woman was gone already and the seat was empty. Ida left the train wondering how long she would have to wait to post a note back to Abram to let him know where he could find her.

CHAPTER EIGHT

If it be possible, as much as lieth in you,
live peaceably with all men.
Romans 12:18

bram returned mid-morning from his morning chores. The cows had been fidgety and impatient after last night's rainstorm, and he wondered if having arrived home a few minutes earlier would have allowed him to intercept Ida. She must've left that morning while he was gone. The note she left propped up on the worn, hand-me-down wooden kitchen table was the only thing left of her.

He'd sunk into a rickety chair on the porch to read her words, feeling a wave of mixed emotions as he read. He felt anger, frustration, relief, and then concern, but mostly relief. It would be easier for him now, wouldn't it? Having a wife and child had been a burden he wasn't sure he was ready for and now, in a matter of hours, its weight had been lifted. That was something to be grateful for, wasn't it? He could get back to his life without Ida, the life he'd been living for years, the one he was accustomed to.

What about my family? What will I tell them?

He already knew what they'd say. He'd get a repeat of the same lecture he'd already heard a hundred times from his father. The one about taking responsibility for his actions, the one about how he needed to be 'a proper man' and make the best of his choices.

And then his mother would have a few words for him too. She'd be disappointed in him; she'd give him that look that only a mother can give, the one that says, 'I raised you to be better than this.' That look alone would send him searching for Ida without delay and, no matter what it took, that look alone would cause him to force Ida back home to him, whether that's what he wanted or not.

The thing that kept rising to the top of all his thoughts had to do with being 'proper man,' like his father always required him of. But this time, it was a different 'proper man' - it was the kind where a grown man decides what's best for that himself and doesn't give in to the coercing of his parents. So, yes, he would be 'proper man' and figure this one out for himself, but that meant he had to take some time. This was the second time Ida had left him. If he fetched her, would there be a third time, and then a fourth? If Ida did not want to live with him, he could not force her.

He wouldn't tell his family Ida had left him. Not yet. In time, when he figured out what *he* wanted, he'd inform them of his decision. He liked the sound of that. *I'll inform them of what's going to happen next when I'm darn well ready to inform them.*

Having reached a decision on his course of action, he hastily ate a simple lunch of bread and cheese, tucked an apple under his arm, and returned to the farm and his chores. He whistled all the way there, as if nothing had happened.

He hadn't counted on how difficult it was going to be to hide the fact that Ida had left until he was ready to reveal it. He hadn't counted on the fact that he'd have to tell a million white lies to hide the truth. He also hadn't counted on how easily those little white lies would come to him.

"No, mother, Ida and I can't come to Sunday lunch this week, Ida needs to rest."

"Oh, Ida's just fine, Mrs. Hammond. Yes, a few of those oranges would be just fine, Ida really likes them."

"Father, I need to get straight home after we finish working on the barn today, I can't go fishing with you today, Ida is expecting me."

"Any letters today, Mr. Postman? Ida is expecting something from her family. No? Nothing today? Okay. I'll check back tomorrow. Ida's really anxious for some news from home."

It got easier and easier to make up reasons why he couldn't do anything except go to work and come home. He was pleased with how maturely he was handling the fact that his wife and unborn child had left him, and how two weeks had passed without anyone suspecting the truth.

And yet, the joy of escaping confrontation with his family was short-lived. He would arrive home from a day in the fields, or from a long day spent patching fences and herding cattle and no one would be there to greet him. The stove was cold. The fresh-baked bread Ida had kept on hand for his suppers had long been eaten, and there was no fresh loaf to take its place. He had no one to talk to at night, no one to help him take off his boots or ask him how his day was. When the sun rose in the mornings, it hit the empty spot on the couch where Ida used to sew. It didn't hit the streaks of gold in her dark hair, and tempt him to reach out and touch them. No one said, 'Goodbye, have a good day, see you at dinner,' when he left early in the morning. His small house was cold, and oh so empty.

Each day he drove his buggy into town to check the post. She had said she would write when she was settled. He diligently looked for her promised note in the mail, each day growing more and more discouraged when it failed to arrive.

As he walked through town, he saw families, lovers, and old couples walking together. Never had he noticed these people before, nothing at least beyond a quick glance and a tip of his hat in greeting. Now he found himself studying them, wondering about them noticing them and how they interacted. He saw how fathers grabbed their children's hands and draped an arm around their wives. They looked so happy that they made him feel alone.

He wondered if Ida also felt alone in her new town, wherever that was. Surely she would have returned to Virginia; that's where she'd been heading the last time she'd left him. *Where was she?* Did she see mothers, fathers and children, and wish she had a family, too? At one point in his life, he had resisted growing up and stepping into the grand responsibility of being a husband and father. But the way these people made it look, it must be a lot of fun because everyone was always smiling and looking happy. He wondered if Ida noticed this too.

She must be so scared; she must feel so alone.

He hit a low point about four weeks after she had left. Lying in bed alone one night, while the rain pelted the shingles of the roof above, Abram thought about how he'd treated Ida, and felt shame. He'd been cruel; he'd made her feel unwanted. He'd made it clear she was infringing on his life and didn't belong in it, and he couldn't blame her for leaving. But in the last few days they'd spent together, he'd tried to be different and he'd tried to change. She really was beautiful, kind, and charming to have around, and he had begun to recognize that. And now, now he would give anything to have her back again.

Just one more chance, Ida? Can I have one more chance? I miss you.

He fell asleep after a long while, and drifted into a dream where he was searching for Ida, high and low, low and high, leaving no stone unturned. He awoke to the sadness that he might never see her again, and had no place to even begin looking for her. *And what if she never writes? What if she doesn't want to be found? Eventually, I will have to tell people what has happened, including my vadder and mudder.*

Expecting nothing and hoping for everything, he visited the post office again that day, as usual.

"Abram, that letter you were asking for, is this it? Came for you today, sir!" The postman handed Abram a slim envelope with the address and his name scrawled in the flowing writing of a feminine hand.

With barely a mumbled thanks, he ripped the envelope from the postmaster's hand and took it outside into the street. Frantically, he opened the envelope; his heart was beating fast. It was from her, from Ida. Inside, all he found was a single sheet of paper. On it was written, *'I am all right.'* Nothing more. No 'come and get me, I miss you,' and no 'I'm sorry that I left.' But still, it was something. It was a starting point. He turned the envelope over. There was no return address, but there was a postmark of Virginia. He had been right; she had gone back to Virginia.

CHAPTER NINE

Now the God of hope fill you with all joy and peace in
believing, that ye may abound in hope,
through the power of the Holy Ghost.
Romans 15:13

awn broke the day after Abram received Ida's note. Abram had been awake most of the night. He struggled to know what to do, not sure if she would want him to fetch her or not. How would he send money to her and the baby if he didn't know where they were?

He weighed what to do in his mind, back and forth. Should he try to find her? Should he wait to go, perhaps until the baby had been born? If he found her, what if she wouldn't see him or talk to him?

By the time he'd finished milking the cows at his parents' farm, he'd made a decision. The way he saw it, this was all part of growing up, and he owed it to himself to go to her and apologize in person. If she didn't want to come back with him, if she didn't want to have anything to do with him, he'd bow out. Of course, part of acting on this decision was going to require him to tell his family what had been going on, and explain why he was going to be gone from the farm while he went in search of Ida.

Even this didn't scare him much now, not as much as it would have a month or so ago. It was simply a detail that had to be taken care of. He'd made his decision, now it was time to inform them.

Instead of going home, he went in search of his father and mother. As expected, they were breaking their fast in the kitchen of the old farmhouse, laughing about something one of them had said, and looking happy together. *That could be Ida and I someday*, he thought.

He stepped into the warm kitchen, and their laughter quickly faded.

"Good morning, Abram. What brings you around this morning? Ida is okay, right?" his father asked.

"We haven't seen her in so long, Abram. Is everything all right?" His mom looked up at him from behind her coffee cup.

"*Jah*, she's fine. Rather, well, I think she's fine. I don't know, I guess, for sure."

"Abram, you're making no sense. What's happened? Where is she?" His mother asked.

"Virginia."

"Virginia?" Abram's parents exclaimed simultaneously.

His dad threw his head back in frustration, rolling his eyes and taking a deep breath, as if talking himself out of giving Abram a piece of his mind. His mother simply sat there, lips pursed together, gathering up the strength to give the 'I'm so disappointed in you' look.

Abram simply watched the two of them, waiting for inspiration to strike, and for the words to come to him. He didn't get the chance, because his father spoke first.

"So, you're going to Virginia to bring her back? That's what you've come to tell us, right?"

"*Jah.*" Abram nodded.

"Good for you, Son. I'm proud of you. See you when you get back," his father said.

Abram nodded, and turned to walk out of the kitchen.

"Oh, Abram? One more thing, take my buggy into town. I'll pick it up later. You'll get to the train station faster that way, might even make the early train. Go on with you now." His father waved a hand as if to nudge him out of the kitchen, and Abram couldn't help but notice the gleam in his parents' eyes. *They're glad I'm going; they're glad I'm being a man about this.*

"Wait, Abram."

Abram had just walked out the front door of his parents' house. He turned around on hearing his mother's voice. "*Jah?*"

"Take this." She pressed a photograph in his hand.

Abram looked down to see his wedding photo. This was the first time he'd seen it. He looked up and nodded a 'thank you' to his mother and headed for the buggy. He'd thought that the photo would have been destroyed. His parents had never had a photograph in their house before Ida had brought their wedding photograph with her.

A DAY LATER, Abram arrived in Virginia. It had been a trip to remember. While he'd hoped to have a quiet ride to himself to think and consider his next steps, he'd been kept company by an older woman. She hadn't been intrusive, not at all, but here and there she'd asked him questions about himself and the purpose of his journey. Being polite, he had answered her.

At one point, he'd considered telling her a lie. It would have been simpler to say that he was traveling to Virginia for business or for a job opportunity. But something about the woman called to him to speak the truth. And though he wasn't a gushing kind of guy, definitely more stoic for the most part, he found himself telling the whole story to this tiny, non-judgmental woman.

He told it all. How he'd met Ida. How he and his

family had treated her. How he'd had a change of heart and realized that actually, he didn't mind having her around, and then how she'd suddenly left. What the last few weeks had been like for him, and how much he missed her. He even told her how he wished he could name the baby 'Abram.'

"You know, dear," the old woman said, "I knew a man like you once. My Christopher was a knuckle-headed farmer. We met at the fairgrounds late one summer. It was love at first sight for us, and before we knew it, we were expecting a baby. We hadn't gone through the traditional hoops to get there either, if you know what I mean."

Abram studied the older woman, a little shocked that she would offer such private details.

The older woman didn't notice Abram's amazement, and she continued, "My parents were heartbroken that Christopher and I weren't married yet, and they rushed us along and made us get married as quick as possible, so people wouldn't talk. Those were tough years for Christopher and I. Summer changes to Fall and then... well, you know. The bloom of a new relationship fades at first, and things usually become bleaker before they become beautiful again. He even ran off for a few years and worked the railroads, while I stayed home with the three babies we had by that point."

"That must have been hard for you," Abram said.

"I was glad to see him go at first; he didn't know how to be a father, and it was easier for me just to do it myself. When he finally did come back three years later, he was ashamed of his absence and asked my forgiveness in a tone of voice that made me think he was concerned that I wouldn't give it. Of course, I did. I'd also had a change of heart during his absence, and I missed him."

"So you forgave him?" Abram asked.

"Yes, yes I did. Then we proceeded to have seven more babies together, for a total of ten, and we lived happily ever after."

"What was your secret? How did you make it work together?"

"Oh, my dear boy, there's no secret. No, I don't know any secret, I only know one thing: folks change, and folks grow, and love takes time. First blushes pass, but if you want to grow old with someone and love them for life, you better start growing."

"I told Ida that. I told her that love takes time."

They'd pulled up into the station a few hours later, and Abram looked out the window to get a first glimpse of the city. Abram stood and was about to ask the old lady if she was getting off too, but he couldn't see her anywhere.

Her advice had resonated with him, and he found himself hoping Ida would forgive him, if he found her. *I don't even know where to start looking though. How will I find her in this big city?*

Abram started by checking into a local hotel. He felt jittery, and expectant, but had nowhere to direct his energy.

Walking the streets of Virginia was an exhilarating experience. There were so many things to see, so many faces to peer into while looking for Ida. *Where should I start?* He was glad for the picture of her that his mother had given him before he left. He could show people the photograph and ask them if they'd seen her.

He started asking around in saloons and dance halls, not wanting to miss a single opportunity to stumble upon her. Nothing. He walked and walked. Dusty and tired, he felt as though he would never be able to find a needle in this haystack.

Dejected and disappointed, he returned to the hotel. He stayed in his room the rest of the night staring at the photo of their wedding. Now, he wished he'd remembered their first wedding. They'd had a second wedding after they had both been baptized, and that was their real wedding, but still he wished he'd remembered their first.

Maybe she would soon send him another letter. *Jah, that's what I'll do*, he thought. Tomorrow was another day, and he would spend it camped out next to the post office. He'd go there every single day until she showed up. She had to show up eventually, right? *For the sake of my longing heart, I hope so.*

CHAPTER TEN

Humble yourselves therefore under the mighty hand of
God, that he may exalt you in due time.
1 Peter 5:6

After a long day camped by the post office, Abram felt irritable and in need of a wash, but he had come all this way to find Ida and that's exactly what he was going to do. After the post office closed its doors for the day, Abram set off to ask around. He could no longer sit in silence and wait for her to appear as he'd done for the best part of the day. The town seemed smaller than when he'd been there on his *rumspringa,* and no longer seemed the carefree place he'd known. Now that he was a father-to-be, this town and its nightlife was no place for his wife or his child.

Abram couldn't help but grind his teeth at the thought of where his life was now compared to how simple and easy it used to be. A year ago, he wouldn't have considered chasing some girl, much less chasing one a whole day's trip away. But here he was going after Ida, and he didn't know why. Why was he in this God-forsaken town looking for a girl who chose to run away from him?

Abram almost turned on his heel back towards the hotel, but something deep inside didn't let him. Despite all the anger and resentment, there was some other emotion inside, one that he wasn't familiar with. That emotion kept him moving forward with his plan of finding Ida. Even though he felt quite angry with Ida for the selfish way she'd run away, he knew he'd forget his anger as soon as he saw her. But for now, he was unable to give his parents the much-needed help on the farm. Abram walked through the middle of town trying to cool his anger down.

That's it! The saloon! Abram remembered that he'd met Ida in one of the saloons, but which one? Abram broke out into a light jog toward the saloon he used to frequent. He thought that would be where she'd be for sure.

Memories of Ida jumped into his mind. The first time he saw her she was wearing purple, black and feathers. Intoxication had robbed him of too many memories of her. She was a beautiful girl, he could not deny that, and undoubtedly that's what drew him to her.

The memories were vague, but now he was in Virginia, his memories of Ida were growing clearer. Maybe she was telling the truth, maybe the baby was his.

Once he stepped into the dimly lit place, he was hit by the pungent stench of stale beer and old liquor. These were the smells of his *rumspringa*. For a second he was tempted to sit at the bar and order a drink, nearly forgetting he had come there looking for Ida.

He looked around the place and, with a casual sweep of his eyes, he saw no sign of her. He even scanned the dancers, but not for his own pleasure. *She won't be dancing in her condition,* he reminded himself.

SAMANTHA PRICE

Frustrated, Abram took a seat, and waved the bartender over.

"What can I do ya fer?" It was Smitty, the bartender. He was a man of well over six feet tall, and nearly as wide. He had a thick handlebar mustache, and always wore the same blue and white striped shirt. A man of his build would come in handy in a place like that, with its regular brawls.

"Hey Smitty, it's Abram."

Smitty studied Abram for a moment. Then he laughed. "Abram. Well, I'll be a son of a gun! I haven't seen you in ages. How have you been? What are you up to these days?"

"I'm fine, Smitty. Thanks for asking. I'm not drinking today. I'm here looking for Ida. Do you remember her?" Abram asked, while taking another look around the saloon.

"Ida, huh? Yeah, you always were sweet on that little ol' thing. And who could blame ya? She was gorgeous! Ah, Ida," Smitty said nostalgically, as if picturing her in that purple and black dress, just the way Abram had been earlier.

Abram frowned, and said, "Yes, Ida. She's my wife

100

now, Smitty, so I'd appreciate it if you wiped that look off your face. We've got a baby on the way for crying out aloud, and I can't find her anywhere."

"Wife? Baby? Why didn't you say something before? Look at you all grown up. Good for you." Smitty held out a large hand for Abram to shake.

Abram shook his hand and pulled Smitty close. "Have you seen her, or haven't you, Smitty?"

Smitty slowly lowered his hand, with a hurt look on his face. "Well, no need to shout there, boy."

Abram hung his head in frustration. "I'm sorry, but I want to find my wife. Have you seen her around here anywhere?"

"Ida?" Smitty asks.

Abram ground his teeth. "Yes, Smitty, Ida. Have you seen her? Has she been in here?"

"Well, no. I can't say I've seen her. And I know I'd remember if I did," he said with a wink, angering Abram even more.

Abram pounded his fist on the bar and then rested his head on his forearm. He had been so sure that he'd find her there. This was their place, the place where they'd met, and the place where she'd worked. Where else would he look?

"Don't you fret, son. We'll find her," Smitty assured Abram, and patted him on the back. He called to the piano player. "Hey, Pete! Have you seen Ida around these parts?"

The musician stopped playing mid-song and looked up. "Ida, the dancer? She's back in town?" he asked, a little too excitedly.

Abram looked over to glare at him, and Smitty explained, "Yessir. This here is her concerned husband. They've got a baby comin' and he can't find her. Has she been in here that you know of?"

"Nah, Smitty. I'd remember if I'd seen her," Pete said with a wink, ignoring the part about Abram being her husband.

Abram made a move to get off the barstool and head towards Pete, but Smitty planted a firm hand on Abram's arm. "He don't mean no harm, boy," Smitty whispered.

Abram sat back down and rested his face in his hands. How could she have left him in the first place? How could she do that to him, seeing as she was expecting his child? If he couldn't find Ida, why would he even go back home? He knew he had to find her. He didn't even know for sure that she was in the town, but it was the only place he knew of that she would go. Besides, the envelope of the letter she'd sent to him had been postmarked as coming from Virginia.

Exhausted, Abram said a quick goodbye to Smitty, and headed back to the hotel. He dragged his feet and hung his head the entire way, partly out of weariness and partly to avoid getting recognized. He was in no mood to chat or reminisce with anyone who might have known him from his previous stay.

He flung the door of his hotel room open, kicked off his boots, and let himself flop onto bed. He fell asleep instantly, but it was not a restful sleep. Abram tossed and turned the entire night, having terrible dreams of losing Ida forever.

Abram woke the morning with a tremendous headache. He contemplated going back to bed, but decided the sooner he started looking for Ida, the sooner he would be bound to find her.

First, Abram headed towards a little restaurant for breakfast. He'd often been to the place, and he was almost certain that he'd been there with Ida. Before he arrived at the restaurant, he could smell the sizzling bacon, which made his stomach grumble with hunger. Once he stepped inside, he went straight up to the counter to enquire about Ida.

"Hello, Miss Chatwood. Your food smells as good as ever, ma'am. How are you this fine morning?" Abram asked politely, being in a much better mood than he'd been the previous night in the saloon.

"Abram King! Oh, it's been much too long since I saw that sweet face." The heavy, middle-aged lady gushed, and pinched his cheeks.

Abram smiled politely. "You're too kind, ma'am. I'm just dying to have some of your delicious cooking, but first I have something to ask you."

"Go right ahead, honey."

"Well, I'm back in town looking for Ida, a girl I knew. I met her at the saloon."

Miss Chatwood interrupted him by saying, "Oh, Ida Fletcher? What a lovely girl."

Abram could feel heat come into his cheeks. "Yes, ma'am, she's beautiful, and she's Ida King now."

"Oh my! You two young ones got hitched? How sweet."

"Yes, ma'am, we did," Abram said. "The thing is, I can't seem to find her, but I know she's in this here town. Have you seen or heard anything, Miss Chatwood?"

"Awe, sweet pea. I'm sorry, but she hasn't been by here," Miss Chatwood said.

Abram felt his stomach drop. He knew she was in the town, but was she hiding from him in case he went to find her? Was she avoiding the obvious places he'd look?

"I'm sorry I couldn't help you find Ida, honey, but would you like some breakfast now? You look like you could use some food in you," Miss Chatwood said, handing him a menu.

Abram took the menu. He wasn't that hungry, but figured he should keep his strength up. "Just give me the bacon and eggs, thanks." He handed the menu back, and took a seat at the nearest table.

He ate his breakfast as fast as he could so he could carry on with his search. Without a clue where to start Abram figured he should go from business to business, and ask if they'd seen her. He had their old wedding photo that Ida had left with his mother. Abram went back to the hotel to fetch the photograph; it might be his key to getting Ida back - he hoped.

Once he had the small photograph in hand, he started at one end of the street and worked his way down. He showed everyone the photograph and asked if they'd seen her recently.

After four days of getting no closer to finding Ida, and nearly running out of money, Abram was becoming genuinely concerned for Ida's wellbeing. If none of the hotels had any record of her, where was she staying? If none of the restaurant owners had seen her, where was she eating? Then his next thought almost made him sick; maybe something bad had happened to her.

Abram hurried to visit every doctor in town, but none had seen her. Now he was worried sick. He was stumbling through a part of town he'd never been to before, when his nose caught a familiar scent of stale beer and liquor. Is that another saloon? He followed the odor, as well as the sounds of laughter and cheers.

Abram wandered into this unfamiliar saloon, with his photograph ready to ask about Ida. He looked around and thought it seemed like a pretty decent place. He walked over to the bar and asked a man drinking, "Whose place is this?"

The man turned slightly on his stool to look at Abram, and said, "Well this ol' place here belongs to Lady Mills."

"Is that Millie Meyers?" Abram asked. He had some vague memory of Ida mentioning a fifty-something-year-old woman who owned a saloon. She'd told him that's the first place she'd ever worked when she arrived in Virginia.

"Yessum. That would be her," the drunken man slurred.

Abram took a seat next to the man, facing away from the bar. At the very same moment, he caught a glimpse of an undeniably expectant young lady racing up the stairs. *It's her. It's Ida!*

Abram sprang to his feet, and called out, "Ida!" He made to go after her when a surprisingly strong woman pulled him back into his seat by his shoulders. Abram turned to find himself face to face with a lady, who he knew must be Lady Mills.

"Hello, Abram. I reckon you're here looking for your wife," she said.

"Yes, ma'am, I am. I know that was her going up those stairs and I intend to follow her."

Lady Mills placed her hands on her hips. She cocked her head at him, and said, "Well, you're going to have to see me about that, now. See, this is my saloon and up those stairs is my home. I've allowed Ida to stay up in my guest room in exchange for her services as a waitress. I love that sweet girl, and I'm not about to let some man go up there and throw mean words around, or empty promises. Especially not with the condition she's in. Now, if you can promise me that there will be no more shouting, and you intend to have a civilized discussion with Ida as husband and wife, I will gladly allow you upstairs to see her. Can you do that for me?"

Abram was stunned at the woman's strong presence and nodded slowly.

"All right then. Get. It's the second door on the right," Lady Mills said, and then walked away from him.

Abram took a moment to compose himself, and then slowly got off the creaky barstool. He took a few unsteady steps towards the staircase, then stopped to take a deep breath. Now that he'd found Ida he had no idea what he would say to her. He knew he had to go up those stairs though. Ida was his wife and she was carrying his unborn child. He ground his teeth. Finally, Abram made it to the stairs and started climbing.

CHAPTER ELEVEN

Deceit is in the heart of them that imagine evil:
but to the counsellors of peace is joy.
Proverbs 12:20

*I*da could hear the door creak open, and she knew it must be Millie coming to check on her. Millie had been so good to her, letting her stay in the guest room and feeding her home cooked meals in return for waiting on a few patrons a day. Millie was a smart woman who'd been quick to pick up on her distress; they'd both spied Abram as soon as he'd come in the Saloon door minutes before. Millie had told her she would handle Abram and had sent her straight up to her room.

Ida hoped Millie was going to make her a nice cup of tea. Ida smiled, and turned her head, about to speak, but it was not Millie standing there.

Ida leaped to her feet, and both hands went straight to her rounded belly. Ida was overcome with conflicting emotions. They stood and stared at each other for more than a moment. Ida hoped for some kind of embrace from her husband after so many days apart, but all she got was an icy look and silence.

Not knowing what else to do, Ida sat down on the edge of the bed, and looked out the window. There was a great view over the town. She watched an elderly couple walking a dog. A tear rolled down her cheek as she felt Abram staring at her. "Say something," Ida pleaded, as she turned to face him.

Abram moved and sat down on the bed next to her, and said, "You're a lot bigger; the *boppli's* growing well."

Ida's eyes fell to the ground. "The baby is just weeks away."

"Come home with me. We can still catch the last train of the day."

"No," Ida said, and looked into Abram's face; he seemed shocked by her refusal.

"Look, I'm sorry. Okay? I apologize for the way I've treated you. It wasn't right. I see that now. And I've come all this way to find you, and now I'm not going back without my wife and child." Abram took Ida's hand in his. "I just want to know you're all right. Let's go home and let me take care of you."

Ida could see that Abram was genuinely concerned for her and the baby, but it was not enough. She shook her head. "I'm just fine right here. Millie is letting me stay almost free until the baby comes, and then I'll work full time for her. I don't need to be taken care of by a man who doesn't love me." Hearing her own words caused tears to flow down her cheeks. She got off the bed and walked away to the other side of the room, too upset to be near him.

"What do you mean 'a man who doesn't love you'?" he asked. "I married you - twice."

Ida cackled and angrily wiped the tears from her face. "It's not like you wanted to," she spat back. "I know you were too drunk to even remember the ceremony. If it weren't for your parents forcing you to stay with me, you'd have been long gone, months ago."

Abram shook his head and jumped to his feet. He took one stride to stand in front of her. She trembled slightly in fear from the fuming look on his face. "What's that got to do with anything?" he yelled. "I'm right here, right now. That's all that should matter."

"No!" she yelled right back, no longer intimidated by him. "That's not all that matters, Abram. A man is supposed to love his wife. You don't love me, Abram, and that matters to me."

Abram stepped away from Ida. The two stood in silence for a few minutes, and then Abram said, "Let's go home, Ida. We can talk about this later. Let's just go home."

Ida crossed her arms in front of her chest. "I am not going anywhere with you unless you can look me in the eye, and tell me in all honesty that you love me, and we will live together normally as man and wife."

"Don't be ridiculous, Ida. You're my wife. You're carrying my baby. We need to go." He walked to the door and opened it wide, gesturing for Ida to walk out in front of him.

Ida went back to the bed and sat down. "Not until you can tell me that you love me."

Abram hung his head. "I came all this way, Ida. Isn't that enough for you? Can't you see how worried sick I've been?"

Ida scoffed. "Yes, Abram. You seemed very worried when you were about to have a drink at the bar. Look, the bottom line is this: we've been married all these months and I'm having your child, but you are yet to just tell me that you love me. That's all I need, and we can be on our way. Until then, I'm not moving."

"I've had enough!" Abram bellowed. "You're my wife and you'll do as I say. Get off that darn bed right now, missy! We are leaving here right now!"

Ida had never seen Abram angry. His face had turned a few shades redder, and there was a vein throbbing in his forehead that she had never seen before. She knew he was good man deep inside, but she also knew that she was a good woman. She deserved to be loved, and she deserved to be treated as though she were loved.

Ida pushed herself carefully off the bed. The two stood and stared at one another. Ida felt a sudden movement in her belly. She broke their intense gaze and looked down at her belly. She placed both hands on her abdomen gently and smiled. She looked up at Abram, and said, "Our baby is moving, Abram. I can feel it. Do you want to touch it?"

Abram looked down at her swollen belly, and then back up at her, and said, "Let's just go home."

Ida's sniffed back her tears as she rubbed her stomach. "No, Abram. My baby and I are staying right here unless you can tell me you love me. Can you?"

Without another word, Abram turned away from his crying wife and walked out the door, shutting it behind him.

Ida was stunned that he couldn't say it. He must love her to come all that way to find her. She loved him, so wouldn't he love her the same? She took a few deep breaths and looked out the window. She didn't cry. She knew that tears wouldn't make Abram love her. That was the end for her and Abram, but she still had her baby. At least she had loved the baby's father. She'd learned about God from Abram's family, and from the community, and that would stay with her forever. She knew that God would always be with her. It said in the Bible that God would never leave her or forsake her. God would be with her through the hard times that might be ahead for her and her baby.

Ida smiled at the thought of always having a part of Abram with her, in their child, and if that were all that she could have, that would have to be enough. The baby would love her even if Abram was not able to.

CHAPTER TWELVE

Blessed are the peacemakers: for they shall be called the children of God.
Matthew 5:9

*A*bram stomped down the stairs. *I've never heard my parents say that they love each other. Why's it so important to hear the words? Of course I love her, she's my wife. I didn't come all this way to fetch her back because I don't love her.* Abram landed on the nearest bar stool. Why was it so important to Ida that he said out aloud that he loved her? The thought of saying the words filled him with uneasiness. They weren't easy words to say when no one had ever said them to him. His parents and his siblings had never expressed their love in such a way; the whole thing of speaking one's feelings out aloud was foreign to him.

Ida wasn't coming with him and he didn't know what to do. Abram had never bargained on Ida saying 'no.' He thought she'd be delighted simply by the fact that he had gone looking for her after the way she'd taken off. He felt like he didn't know anything anymore, just that he needed a drink, or two. At that moment he didn't care about the community, the *Ordnung* or *Gott*. He needed to get drunk to take the pain away. He caught the eye of the bartender and summoned him over.

"What can I do for you, son?" the bartender asked.

"Whiskey," Abram said.

The bartender grabbed a glass for him, but Abram stopped him. "No, a bottle."

The bartender raised his eyebrows, but did as he was told. He grabbed a nearly full bottle of whiskey off the shelf and handed it to Abram, who placed money on the bar. Abram took the bottle and turned toward the door, but before he could get to it, Millie stood in his path.

"Let me go, Millie. She doesn't want to go home with me," Abram said.

"And how is that bottle there going to fix that?" she asked.

"It's not," Abram said, and pushed past her. He walked out of the saloon and let out a long, sad sigh. He decided to head out of town a bit. As he walked away, he remembered a spot by a creek he used to go to with his friends when he was on *rumspringa.* It was a perfect place for him to go, because there were no memories of Ida there.

Abram made it to the creek, and he could almost hear his friends' laughter. It all seemed so long ago now. Now he was married and about to be a father. He ground his teeth at the thought - just like he always had. He took a huge swig from the bottle of whiskey, and it burned his throat. He listened to the creek babble for a minute, and then raised the bottle to his lips again.

Instead of taking another drink, Abram launched the bottle as hard as he could across the creek. The force spun him around so fast he fell to his knees. *I don't need drink; I only need Gott. Dear Heavenly Father, help me sort out this mess I've gotten myself into. I do love Ida, but I can't make myself say it.*

Millie had been right; drinking wasn't going to help get Ida back, but he didn't know what would. Abram dug his hands into the wet dirt, and let out a yell that had been building up since he arrived in Virginia. He yelled like he'd never yelled before. He grabbed fistfuls of dirt and flung them at a tree. He rolled around on the ground, and then sat for a moment to catch his breath. Then, he kicked off his boots and dipped his toes into the cool, refreshing creek.

Abram sat like that for a few minutes, not thinking about anything, just surrounded by the sounds of nature. The peace of God filled his heart and his mind. Finally, he allowed his mind to wander, and it went right to Ida. He shook the thought of her from his head. Instead, he decided to think about what he wanted from life.

He was a man now, and his days of fooling around with his friends were over, but what now? Abram was as confused as ever. Why couldn't Ida just have gone home with him? Abram realized that he did want to go home, and have Ida go with him, and not because that's what his parents or the community would want. He wanted Ida with him for good.

All this, coming to this town and trying so hard to find her, it's all been because she's exactly what I want. I want her to be a part of my life. I can't go home without her.

He was scared about becoming a father, but it was what he wanted. He wanted Ida, himself, and their baby to be a family.

The more Abram thought about it, the more he realized that it was absolutely true. That was the first time he had ever thought about being a husband and father without grinding his teeth. That's exactly what he wanted, but he'd been running away from it the whole time. He'd been holding Ida at arm's length since the beginning, because he felt trapped by their sudden marriage, and her sudden appearance at his parents' house. But now, he could see that he was never trapped at all. Ida and a family were exactly what he wanted.

It had taken Ida running away, and almost losing her, for him to realize what he wanted. He finally knew what he wanted, and was going to get it. Abram leaped to his feet and rushed to put his boots back on. He ran back into town as fast as he could. It was late, and he didn't want Ida to fall asleep before he could get back.

Abram burst through the doors of Lady Mills' saloon and raced up the stairs without asking her permission. "Ida. Ida, it's Abram!" he called out on his way to her bedroom.

He flung open her door without knocking, and Ida stood before him framed by the soft light of a lamp near her window. Abram walked up to her and gently wrapped his arms around her. He felt a little resistance at first, but he didn't care. He was just happy just to be near her, to smell her hair, and to feel her soft heartbeat against his chest.

"Have you been drinking?"

He finally pulled away, and looked her in the eyes. "Ida, I'm sorry for everything I have put you through since the day we got married. You deserve so much better, and if you'll just come home with me, I will be the best husband I can be. I'm going to spend the rest of my life taking care of you, and making you happy. Just come home with me please?" Tears fell from Abram's eyes. "I need you to come home and be with me." Abram took both of Ida's hands in his own, and looked deep into her eyes, not caring that tears were falling down his cheeks.

"Abram, I can't. I ..."

Abram held a finger up to her lips, took a deep breath, closed his eyes, and said softly, "I love you, Ida." As soon as he said the words, he looked at her to see tears form in her eyes. He placed a hand on her belly. "I love you both."

Ida smiled and relaxed against his body while his arms wrapped around her. "The baby's kicking; the baby heard your voice."

Abram took a step back, and placed his warm hand on her belly once more. He smiled, happy for the first time in a long time, and planted a tender kiss on Ida's lips. "I love you," he said again, and this time it felt less strange.

Ida smiled, and tears of joy fell from her eyes, as she said, "I love you, too."

"Then, you will come back with me?"

Ida nodded.

He held Ida tightly in his arms. "We will live as a proper *mann* and *fraa,* and I will make you a happy woman. *Denke* for forgiving me and giving me another chance."

"I'm sorry for running away, again."

"*Nee*, you made me see what a fool I've been. You needed to go away, so I could see what I'd lost. I will make sure that you never think of running away again."

THREE WEEKS LATER, Abram Benjamin King was born in his parents' small cottage at the edge of his grandparents' farm. When he turned two, a sister was born, and then two years after that, a brother arrived. Their household was a happy one from the day that Abram and Ida returned from Virginia, and Ida and Abram would often laugh at how silly they had been in their younger days. Even though their start had been a rocky one, they were grateful that *Gott* had brought them together.

A new commandment I give unto you, as I have loved you,
That ye love one another;
that ye also love one another.
John 13:34

FROM THE AUTHOR

Thank you for reading Amish Baby Surprise. I hope you enjoyed it. To stay up to date with my new releases and special offers, add your email at my website in the newsletter section.
https://samanthapriceauthor.com/
Blessings,
Samantha Price

ABOUT SAMANTHA PRICE

USA Today Bestselling author, Samantha Price, wrote stories from a young age, but it wasn't until later in life that she took up writing full time. Formally an artist, she exchanged her paintbrush for the computer and, many best-selling book series later, has never looked back.

Samantha is happiest on her computer lost in the world of her characters. She is best known for the Ettie Smith Amish Mysteries series and the Expectant Amish Widows series.

www.SamanthaPriceAuthor.com

Samantha loves to hear from her readers. Connect with her at:

samantha@samanthapriceauthor.com

www.facebook.com/SamanthaPriceAuthor

Follow Samantha Price on BookBub

Twitter @ AmishRomance

Instagram - SamanthaPriceAuthor

CPSIA information can be obtained
at www.ICGtesting.com
Printed in the USA
LVHW081507020420
652016LV00018B/1585

9 781512 218299